# 5 Minute
# FARMYARD
## TALES

# Welcome to Windytop Farm!

There's always something happening down on the farm
when these friends get together!

Duchess

Farmer Barnes    Annie    Harold

Pompom

Delilah

Cackle

Biggy Pig

Lala Lamb

Busy Hen

Denby Dog    Pup    Dymphna    Mrs. Speckles

# 5 MINUTE
# FARMYARD
## TALES

WRITTEN BY NICOLA BAXTER
ILLUSTRATED BY JENNY PRESS

ARMADILLO

This edition printed in 2007

© 1999 Bookmart Limited

ISBN: 978-1-84322-116-6

3 5 7 9 10 8 6 4 2

Published by Armadillo Books
an imprint of Bookmart Limited
Registered Number 2372865
Blaby Road
Wigston, Leicester
LE18 4SE

Printed in Thailand

# Contents

# Sweet Dreams, Harold!

When you have a warm, dry stable, filled with fresh, golden straw, and your tummy is full of oats and carrots and other good things, you should be able to get a good night's sleep—if you're a horse, of course! But poor old Harold, who had lived on Windytop Farm for a very long time, now spent all *day* dozing in the sun.

"It's because he's getting old," whispered Cackle the rooster. But a rooster's whisper, as you may know, is not very quiet. Old Harold raised his sleepy head and said, "No, it's not, Cackle. It's because I can't get a wink of sleep at night."

"Why not?" asked Busy Hen. "You've got a lovely stable. It's much nicer than our henhouse. I've often told Cackle."

"It's not that," yawned Harold. "It's the noise at night. It's terrible!"

Cackle started to strut about. "I do *not* make a noise in the night," he crowed. "I wait until it's almost, almost daybreak. I do! I do!"

"Nobody said it was you, Cackle," clucked Busy Hen. "Your crowing is beautiful. I believe it's those mice. Am I right, Harold?"

"Quite right," agreed the old horse. "They are scritch-scratching all night long. Some noises can be ignored— like the wind in the trees, or the rain on the roof. But you can't ignore scritch-scratching. You just can't."

"Leave it to me," said Busy Hen. And later in the day she went to Harold's stable and had a very long conversation with a little person with a twitchety nose and a long tail.

A week later, Harold was trotting about the farmyard as usual, much to everyone's delight. And Busy Hen was as proud as punch of the brand new henhouse she shared with Cackle and the other hens.

"I knew Farmer Barnes wouldn't leave us in that old henhouse once it had mice in it," she clucked. "And those mice just love their new home—so everyone's happy!"

7

# The Cluckety Duck

Farmer Barnes' duckpond was never a very peaceful place. Hardly a day went by when there was not some kind of squawking and squabbling among the reeds. Those ducks were always making a noise. Sometimes it was because Carter Cat was prowling too close to their nests on the bank. Sometimes it was because Dymphna, their leader, had eaten almost all the lovely slimy weed at one end of the pond. Sometimes it was just because ducks love to hear the sound of their own voices.

One day, Farmer Barnes brought a new duck to the pond.

"Be nice to her, you daffy ducks," he said. "She's lived all by herself with an old lady for a long, long time. She's not used to your quacky, splashy ways."

For several days, the little duck paddled shyly around the pond and didn't say a word. The other ducks, who did their best to be kind, thought she must be shy. At last Dymphna, who was curious about the newcomer, waddled up and asked her how she was finding her new home.

The duck looked up and opened her beak. She said her first word on Windytop Farm. It was … *"Cluck!"*

For a moment, Dymphna thought her ears must be full of pond mud. But the little duck spoke again. "Cluck!" she said. "Cluck, cluckety, cluck!"

Dymphna was so surprised that she sat down *plop!* on her newly curled tail feathers. Whoever heard of a clucking duck? And the trouble was that none of the ducks could understand a word she clucked.

Dymphna knew that she would have to talk to Busy Hen. It was well known that Busy Hen knew several foreign languages, but Dymphna and Busy Hen were not the best of friends.

Later that day, the farmyard animals saw Busy Hen deep in conversation with the newcomer, fluffing her feathers and chatting as if they had been friends for years.

"It's quite simple," she told Dymphna that evening. "This little duck is an orphan. She was brought up by an old lady's French hen. So of course, she has never learned to speak duck language. We will have to teach her."

The new duck, whose name was Daphne, was a very quick pupil. How proud of her Dymphna and Busy Hen were when she first dived into the pond with a loud, "QUACK!"

I'm afraid the duckpond is noisier than ever these days!

# Biggy Pig's Problem

Biggy Pig was the oldest pig on Windytop Farm and he was also the biggest. That, of course, was how he got his nickname, for his real name was Brewster Barnstaple Buddleham Pride. Somehow, Biggy Pig sounded a lot more friendly, and Biggy was certainly a friendly pig.

One day, Farmer Barnes leaned over Biggy Pig's sty and scratched his back with a stick.

"Old friend," he said, "there's a very important day coming up for you on Friday. I want you to eat as much as you can, so that you're as big and fat as can be."

Although Biggy Pig snorted happily at Farmer Barnes, he was rather quiet for the rest of the day.

"What's the trouble, Biggy?" asked Harold the horse. "You seem to be off your fodder, old friend."

Biggy gulped. I'm very much afraid," he said, "that I won't need fodder where I'm going. Farmer Barnes wants me to look as big and fat as I can for Friday. I think he means to take me to the market."

Harold looked serious. "That's terrible, Biggy," he said. "There's only one thing you can do. Diet! No one takes a thin pig to market."

So for the next few days, Biggy hardly touched his food. And Farmer Barnes was worried about him. But still, when Friday came, he loaded Biggy up into the trailer and set off for town.

"Farewell, old friends!" called Biggy, with a lump in his throat, as the farmyard animals lined up to wave goodbye.

But Biggy was in for a surprise. Farmer Barnes didn't take him to the market at all. He took him to the County Show, where Biggy Pig, in spite of his diet, looked as fat and handsome as any pig you have ever met. You should have seen how proud he looked as he arrived back at the farm—with his First Prize ribbon!

# Where's That Goat?

Scraggles the goat had lived on Windytop Farm almost as long as Biggy Pig. But unlike Biggy, he was not popular with the other animals. The fact was you just couldn't trust Scraggles. Even if he *knew* he had found your best straw hat or your special store of apples, he would still eat them. He just couldn't help himself. To a goat, almost everything looks like food. In fact, almost everything *is* food.

"I wouldn't mind," said Harold the horse, "but that was my very best bridle—the one I wear for giving children rides at the local show. And it was so tough and chewy, I can't believe he enjoyed it."

"That's the trouble with goats," said Biggy Pig. "They've got such enormous appetites." (Although Biggy Pig could eat for a week without stopping, he did draw the line at hats and bridles.)

"Isn't there something we can do?" clucked Busy Hen. "I can't bear to lose another lovely nest of straw. Isn't there something we can do to stop that wretched goat?"

"No, my dear," crowed Cackle the rooster. "I'm afraid goats will be goats." And that really was the wisest thing that Cackle, who was not known for his brains, had ever said.

But as things turned out, the animals didn't have to do anything. Scraggles did it all by himself. One breezy morning, when the sun was shining, he took a liking to Farmer Barnes' laundry, flapping and flipping in the wind. He munched through three pairs of socks, the bottom half of a pair of pyjamas, half a shirt, two pillowcases, and several pairs of … well, *underwear*. He was just starting to nibble a delicious-looking vest, when Farmer Barnes came back to the farmhouse for his lunch.

Oh dear! There was roaring and raging, shouting and stamping. And Farmer Barnes went straight to his workshop to find a stout chain and an even stouter stake.

Now Scraggles has to content himself with a fresh patch of grass every day. And the cow called Duchess has a brand new hat with no bites out of it at all.

# Busy Hen's Chicks

One spring day, Busy Hen sat down on her nest and stayed there. She didn't get up to scratch in the dust, or cluck at Dymphna Duck, or tell everyone on the farm just what she thought about any subject that came into her head. No, she simply sat.

Of course, all the animals knew what *that* meant. Busy Hen was going to hatch out some chicks, as she did every year at this season.

"How many will it be this time, Busy Hen?" called Harold the horse as he clip-clopped by on his way to the meadow.

Busy Hen put her head under her feathers and counted. "Ten and then some more," she said at last. Hens are not very good at counting, although they are excellent with foreign languages.

Even for Busy Hen, that was a lot of eggs, but she was determined to hatch out every one of them, one day soon.

And sure enough, the morning came when Busy Hen heard a tap-tap-tapping from under her feathers. Pretty soon, the sweetest little chick you've ever seen popped his head out of his egg. Before long, his twelve little brothers and sisters popped their heads out too. Busy Hen cuddled them close under her wings and smiled. She didn't sleep a wink all night, as she guarded her precious babies.

But next morning, the little chicks became restless. First one and then another popped out from under Busy Hen's feathers and wobbled off on spindly legs to explore the world.

"Help!" called Busy Hen. She didn't know what to do. Thirteen chicks were just too many. If she ran after one of them, another two escaped in the opposite direction. If she kept five of them warm under her wings, the other eight wandered out of the henhouse and got their feet cold.

It wasn't until Biggy Pig suggested a babysitting service that Busy Hen heaved a sigh of relief. Each little chick found itself with an extra special aunt or uncle.

"How about your usual six chicks next year, Busy Hen?" suggested Harold, as he puffed after his special nephew.

But Busy Hen smiled to herself and put up her scrawny feet. As everyone knew, numbers were not her strong point…

# Little Lala Lamb

When the snow was lying thick on the ground at Windytop Farm, Farmer Barnes set off to find his sheep.

The snow had come just when he was expecting the sheep to start having their lambs, and he was afraid the little ones would not survive the bitter cold.

You can imagine how relieved he was to find the sheep sheltering behind a wall. And none of them had yet had their lambs.

"Come on, my old dears," said the farmer. "You come with me to my warm barn. It's too cold for you out here."

But when the farmer had shepherded all the woolly animals into his biggest barn, he counted them to make sure they were all there. They weren't. One sheep was missing.

Farmer Barnes turned his coat collar up and went out into the cold one more time. Snow was flying all around him, and he could hardly see where he was going.

Out on the hill once more, the farmer searched behind every sheltering wall and under every bare-branched tree. He was cold and hungry, but still he searched on.

At last, just as he thought he would have to turn back, he heard, above the wind, a little sound. He stood very still and listened. It sounded—yes, it really did—it sounded like someone singing, right by his feet!

Farmer Barnes bent down and began to dig with his bare hands. Just below the surface he came upon two bright little eyes—and then two more! The missing sheep had had her lamb, and it was the little lamb who was singing, buried in the snow.

The happy farmer tucked the lamb into his coat and helped her mother up. Then the three set off, back to the farmyard.

"I'm going to call you Lala," Farmer Barnes told the warm little lamb under his coat. "Because if you hadn't sung your lala song, you and your mother might never have come safely home."

# Farmer Barnes' Apple Pie

One summer, Farmer Barnes bought a pair of geese. They were beautiful white birds who honked when anyone came near them.

"There have been a lot of burglaries around here," the farmer told them. "Your job is to warn me if any strangers come to Windytop Farm. In return, you can run about in my lovely orchard all day long."

The geese honked as if they understood, and Farmer Barnes went happily back to his work.

And the geese proved their worth much sooner than Farmer Barnes could have imagined. The very next day, when the farmer was away cutting barley, two men drove into the farmyard in a battered old truck.

They skulked around the farmyard for a while, checking that no one was about, then they hurried over to the pigsty and started scooping up the new little piglets.

Of course, the piglets squealed, but that was nothing to the noise the geese made in the nearby orchard. They honked and spread their wings. And they ran so quickly towards the rickety fence that they broke right through it and came rushing into the farmyard, where the men were just loading the last little piglet into the back of their truck.

But at the sight of the geese, the men dropped the last piglet and ran for their lives. The first goose just had time to bite a big hole in the second man's trousers before the truck rumbled into life and revved out of the farmyard with the piglets tumbling one by one out of the open back doors.

Farmer Barnes had heard the commotion even from the other side of the farm. He was very, very pleased as he put the piglets back in their sty and mended the rickety fence.

But when autumn came, and the orchard was full of beautiful apples, Farmer Barnes found that he had a problem. Those geese were used to their orchard and wouldn't let him in! If he so much as approached the gate, they hissed and honked and spread their wings menacingly.

Farmer Barnes was a fair man. "Okay," he said, "you keep my farm safe night and day. I reckon you deserve some rosy apples, and I can go without my apple pie—this time!"

19

# Duchess and Delilah

**W**hen the farm animals saw Duchess the cow with a pretty young calf by her side one morning, they were surprised.

"I didn't know she was expecting a *baby*!" hissed Dymphna to the other ducks. When Duchess was going to have a baby she looked as round and rolling as a barrel. No one had noticed any difference in the cow's trim figure. It was very strange.

Even more strange was the way Duchess treated her calf. She did her best to ignore it. Usually, she was the first to show off her new offspring to the whole farmyard. This time she was very off-hand about the whole thing.

"Oh that," she said to Busy Hen, when she clucked an inquiry. "Yes, she is a pretty calf, I guess, though her feet are big."

"So she *is* your calf?" asked Busy Hen, determined to get to the bottom of the matter.

"You could say that," said Duchess carelessly.

It took over a week for the story to come out. The calf came from a nearby farm, and Farmer Barnes had agreed to look after her.

"Duchess," he had said to his most motherly cow, "this little calf's mamma can't look after her, so I want you to do it. You'll take care of her so well."

Duchess did try to be kind to the little calf. She made sure she had sweet milk to drink and the warmest place in the cowshed to sleep. But somehow Duchess just couldn't warm to her new daughter.

"I can't forget that she isn't really my own calf," she confessed to Busy Hen, "and I'm not really her mother. What's more, she's called Delilah. Such a silly name!"

The little calf turned out to be very adventurous. Duchess found she had to spend more and more time rescuing her from difficult situations. And Duchess grumbled to all the animals, until they were really fed up.

Then, one day, the little calf got into real trouble. There was a commotion from the duckpond and a frightened cry from the calf. She had fallen into the water, but she hadn't learned to swim! Oh, no!

While all the animals were wondering what to do, Duchess plunged into action. She strode into the pond, grabbed the little calf by her tail, and hauled her out of the water. She was beaming with happiness as she licked the calf's face dry.

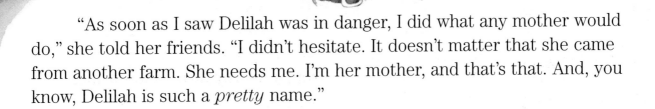

"As soon as I saw Delilah was in danger, I did what any mother would do," she told her friends. "I didn't hesitate. It doesn't matter that she came from another farm. She needs me. I'm her mother, and that's that. And, you know, Delilah is such a *pretty* name."

# A Stitch in Time

Busy Hen was not usually afraid to speak her mind, but there were some subjects that even she felt were a little delicate. She confided in her best friend, Mrs. Speckles.

"Surely someone else has noticed?" she clucked. "I don't like to say anything, but really something should be done."

"My dear, to what do you refer?" asked Mrs. Speckles, leaning a little closer. She liked to speak in what she thought was a fancy way, which always annoyed Busy Hen.

"If you haven't noticed, I'm not sure I can tell you," clucked that lady, carelessly pecking at a piece of straw.

"Busy Hen!" cried Mrs. Speckles, dropping her fancy voice in her eagerness to find out what the mystery was. "We've been friends for umpteen years. If you can't tell *me*, who can you tell?"

Busy Hen knew she was right. "It's Farmer Barnes," she said, without any more delay. "Or rather … it's Farmer Barnes' *trousers*!"

"Aaah," said Mrs. Speckles wisely. She knew exactly what Busy Hen was talking about now. Earlier in the week, Farmer Barnes had torn the seat of his trousers on some thorns, and ever since, although he seemed not to notice, you could see a large portion of his underwear!

"You're quite right, my dear," said Mrs. Speckles. "And I can guess what you're thinking. If you and I and some of the other ladies paid Farmer Barnes a little visit one night…?"

"Exactly," agreed Busy Hen. "How about tonight?"

And that is why, late that night, while Farmer Barnes snored in his bed, Busy Hen and Mrs. Speckles and some of their friends hopped in through the window and got to work with needles, thread, and a piece of Harold's oldest blanket.

Next morning, Farmer Barnes appeared in his repaired trousers in all their glory. But he seemed to notice the patch no more than he had the hole!

"Ladies," said Busy Hen, "we did a fine job, but dear old Farmer Barnes needs a wife. I'm surer of it every day."

The other hens clucked their agreement, and I'm afraid, when Busy Hen makes up her mind about something, it is almost sure to happen!

23

# Harold Saves the Day

Some of the smaller animals were covering their ears on Windytop Farm. Farmer Barnes was red in the face and shouting—and some of his language really wasn't fit for little ears to hear.

Everyone knew their dear old farmer wasn't really furious with his old tractor, even if he did give it a kick with his boot from time to time. He was just annoyed that he couldn't set off to work the bottom field as he had planned. The tractor just wouldn't start.

The animals knew that the tractor was ancient and that Farmer Barnes only kept it because he was fond of it. He could remember his father teaching him to drive it when he was a boy.

"He has that brand new shiny one," crowed Cackle to Biggy Pig. "Why can't he use that?"

Biggy Pig sighed. "Because, Cackle," he said, "the old tractor is standing right in front of the barn so the new tractor can't get out. Anyone can see that."

"Can't he push it out of the way?" asked Cackle.

"You try," suggested Biggy Pig. And I'm afraid that Cackle really has no brains at all, because he did!

When Farmer Barnes had shooed Cackle, who was also very red in the face now, away, he stomped into the house to call the mechanic. The animals could hear his conversation through the open door.

"What? *What?* Not until tomorrow? That's ridiculous! Oh, okay, I understand. See you then."

Poor Farmer Barnes came out of the house and looked hopelessly at the tractor. He sat down on the doorstep and buried his head in his hands. Just then, he heard a friendly clip-clopping noise. It was Harold.

The farmer looked up as the old horse nuzzled the top of his head with his nose. All at once, a smile came over the farmer's face.

"Harold!" he cried. "How do you feel like some work? Like in the old days?"

In no time, the farmer had harnessed Harold to the old tractor. Then he stood by his head and whispered a few encouraging words as Harold began to pull.

Cackle was so impressed by Harold's strength that he fell off his perch. And as the tractor rolled out of the way, *everyone* cheered.

# The Paint Problem

One fine, still day, Farmer Barnes decided to do something he had put off for a long time. There was always so much to do on the farm he never had time to pay attention to the farmhouse. Now the paintwork was looking very shabby. It was time to give the doors and windows a new lick of paint.

Unfortunately, Farmer Barnes was not a man who enjoyed spending money. "Waste not, want not," was his motto. Did he go down to the store in town to buy a couple of large tins of paint? No, he did not. He went into his old workshop behind the henhouse and rummaged about until he found eleven—yes, eleven—cans of old paint. There was some red, some orange, a brilliant turquoise, white, a lot of green, some black, a tiny bit of silver, a pale yellow, two tins of dark brown, and a very vivid violet.

"He can't really be thinking of using all of them," hissed Biggy Pig to Cackle. "It's going to look *awful*!"

"All he's worried about," said Dymphna the duck, "is whether it will keep the wet out. Honestly! As if a little wet ever hurt anyone!"

Meanwhile, Farmer Barnes was scratching his head over the paint cans. He couldn't decide which to start with. It was just at this moment that Annie, who came to collect the eggs, drove into the farmyard. She was a comfortable-looking lady with hair that never seemed to stay where it was put and clothes that looked almost as old as Farmer Barnes'.

"Afternoon, Fred," she called. "What are you doing?"

Farmer Barnes pointed to the paints and explained the problem.

Now even Annie could see that it was not a good idea to paint a house using ten different paints. As was her way, she told Farmer Barnes exactly what she thought about the matter. And she told him straight. By the time she drove out of the yard with the eggs, Farmer Barnes was feeling pretty foolish. How everyone would have laughed at him if he had really painted his house like a rainbow! Still … the paint was too good to waste.

It was then that the farmer had his brilliant idea. He fetched one of Biggy's old water troughs and poured every drop of paint into it. Then he stirred it together with a big stick. There was plenty of paint for all the woodwork on the house. And it was all the same—a sludgy, muddy shade of brown.

When the house was painted, the animals shuddered in horror. It looked terrible. But Dymphna sighed a sigh of pure happiness. "Beautiful," she said. "As I always say, you can't beat mud, can you?"

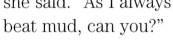

27

# Windy Windytop

There's a reason why Windytop Farm is called Windytop Farm. Most of it is on top of a hill, for one thing, and it's very, very windy for another. Farmer Barnes had been careful to place all the animals' homes so that their doorways pointed away from the wind. But even so, sheds and stables always seem to have little chinks and crannies where the wind can whistle through. And you can always rely on the wind to find them.

One windy day, when Cackle had been blown off his perch on the henhouse roof for the fourth time, Duchess the cow called the animals together for a serious talk.

"This wind is getting worse," she said. "I can't remember it ever being as bad as this when I was young. I put it down to the windmills."

"What windmills?" asked Biggy Pig. "There are no windmills." He sometimes felt that Duchess was talking in riddles.

"Exactly!" cried Duchess eagerly. "In the old days there were windmills to use up the wind. Now it can just blow free."

There was silence for a moment, while everyone decided whether to laugh or not. Then Lala Lamb piped up in her clear, high voice.

"And sailing ships," she said. "There used to be lots of big sailing ships—you know, with sails—to use up the wind, as well."

Biggy Pig felt that the conversation was getting out of hand (or out of trotter, I should say). "Never mind *why* there's more wind," he said, "we've got to find a better way of dealing with it."

Just then one of Farmer Barnes' sheets, which he had put on the line to dry in the wind, flapped past. It had escaped!

Without thinking for a moment what he was doing, Biggy Pig grabbed the passing sheet with two trotters—and took off! The world's first hang-gliding pig sailed over the farmyard, having the time of his life.

"And they say pigs may fly!" Dymphna sniffed. But Duchess was all eagerness. "At least he's using up the wind!" she cried. "Come on everyone! There are lots more sheets on the line!"

Busy Hen covered her eyes with her wings. Someone was sure to get hurt. But whether Biggy Pig was using up the wind, or whether it just dropped of its own accord, the day was suddenly very still.

All the animals were disappointed, except Biggy Pig, who had had a wonderful time, even if he hadn't planned on a water landing!

# Mrs. Marchant's Visit

**F**armer Barnes didn't have many visitors. It wasn't because he was an unfriendly man. It was simply that he hardly ever had time to do anything other than work on the farm. So when he started tidying up the yard one day, the animals got very excited.

"Someone's coming, mark my words," said Busy Hen. "The last time he did this was when his sister from Australia came."

"Maybe he's found a wife," said Dymphna, hopefully.

"But he hasn't met anyone," replied Busy Hen impatiently. She always found Dymphna annoying.

"Well, I don't know how it is with humans. He might have been able to ring up and order one," protested Dymphna. "Like he does the chicken feed, you know."

Busy Hen stalked off in disgust. Dymphna really had no grasp of the real world. "Too much time in the water," muttered the hen. "Her brain's gone soggy."

The animals didn't have long to
wait for the visitor. Two days later,
a shiny car swept into the yard.
A lady got out and walked
delicately across to the
farmhouse on her high heels,
watching all the time to see if she
was stepping in anything messy.

Before the lady even reached the farmhouse, Farmer
Barnes came out. He was wearing his old suit.

"Mr. Barnes, how do you do?" said the
lady. "Will you show me around?"

"Mrs. Marchant? Please come
right this way," replied the farmer.

"He likes her," squealed
Dymphna, jumping up and
down. "She's going to be
Mrs. Barnes!"

"Be quiet, Dymphna!"
whispered Busy Hen.
"She's here for *business*.
Anyone can see that."

Dymphna wasn't
sure what business
was, so she crept
around the pond
to a place where
she could watch
through the weeds.

"I think we can agree your loan," said Mrs. Marchant, as
she climbed back into her car.

Dymphna trotted back and reported to the other
animals. "She's not going to marry him," she said sadly. "She
said, 'I think we can agree you're alone.'"

Busy Hen sighed. She would have to explain to the other
animals later that Farmer Barnes' loan for the new barn was
his only business with Mrs. Marchant.

# Little Pig Gets Lost

Although there were lots of piglets on Windytop Farm, one in particular caught Farmer Barnes' eye. Like his great uncle, Biggy Pig, he had all the signs of being a champion, and Farmer Barnes did like to win ribbons at the County Show. He called the piglet Little Pig. Of course, like Biggy, Little Pig had a long, grand name as well, but no one could ever remember what it was.

Farmer Barnes wanted Little Pig to grow big and fat, like you-know-who, but Little Pig surprised everyone by wanting to do sports! He liked to go for a run every morning and to find lots of time for jumping and diving practice.

"He'll never put weight on at this rate," said Biggy Pig, shaking his head.

Then, one day, Little Pig went missing. At first everyone thought he had gone for a longer run than usual, but when he didn't come back by lunchtime, and his feed trough was still full, all the animals began to get worried.

"He is only a little pig," said Duchess the cow. "He's not old enough to look after himself in the big, wide world."

"We need to search the farm," said Biggy. "The sheep can look in the meadows. I'll check the barns. The hens and ducks can look along the hedges and bushes. And you, Duchess, can wait here in case Little Pig comes home. I do hope he hasn't come to any harm."

But an hour later, the animals returned to the yard without Little Pig. They were now very worried indeed. They sat together, trying to think of a new plan. It was just then that Biggy's sharp ears heard a little squealing sound.

Hardly able to believe their eyes, the animals looked up, and up, and up … right to the top of the tree. A little pink face looked down at them. "I was climbing," said Little Pig, "but I got stuck!"

Busy Hen and Dymphna soon fluttered about and guided Little Pig down. He was very grateful

You know, after that, Little Pig wasn't quite so keen to test his sporting abilities.

"If you keep snuffling in your feed trough like that," said Busy Hen, "you'll soon be even bigger than Biggy Pig!"

And he was!

# Cackle Crows Again

One morning, the sun was already high in the sky when Farmer Barnes came stomping out of the farmhouse.

"I don't know what's the matter with me," he muttered. "I don't think I've ever woken up late before. Poor old Duchess will be wondering where I am."

The first thing Farmer Barnes did every morning was to milk Duchess the cow. He expected to see her waiting at the gate, anxiously looking out for him. He was amazed to see that Duchess was fast asleep under a tree, with Delilah snuggled next to her.

It was the same when Farmer Barnes finished the milking and went to feed Biggy Pig. Biggy was a pig who liked his breakfast—and his lunch, and his supper, and several little snacks in between—so the farmer was surprised to find Biggy snoring in a corner instead of tapping his trotters impatiently on his sty.

Farmer Barnes hurried off to check on the other animals. All of them were sleeping peacefully. The puzzled farmer was just about to telephone the vet to tell him that there was a bad case of sleeping sickness on the farm, when it struck him that all the animals seemed quite well as soon as they were awakened. Then, all of a sudden, he realized what the problem was. Every creature on the farm, including Farmer Barnes, was awakened each morning by Cackle the rooster, crowing at the top of his voice. This morning, Cackle simply hadn't crowed!

When Farmer Barnes finally found Cackle hiding in a corner of the barn, he couldn't help laughing. As usual, Cackle had been poking his beak into places he shouldn't. Farmer Barnes had left a bucket of tar, which he had been using to mend the barn roof, behind the farmhouse. Before it had cooled and dried, Cackle had let his curiosity get the better of him Now he couldn't open his beak to cackle, crow or peck at his breakfast.

So Farmer Barnes called the vet after all. He was soon able to clean up the silly bird and give him a good talking-to about how important it was to brush his beak after every meal.

And for a whole week after that, neither Farmer Barnes nor the rest of the animals grumbled and groaned when Cackle began to crow at the crack of dawn. They didn't even complain when he gave them extra-early double crowing to celebrate being able to open his beak!

# Mrs. Speckles and the Cat

When Mrs. Speckles is upset about something, *everyone* knows it. That hen can make even more noise and fuss than Cackle. *Cluck! Cluck! CLUCK!* She flutters and flaps her way around the farm, making sure no one is in any doubt about what is bothering her.

One morning, Mrs. Speckles was more upset than usual.

"It's that cat!" she cried. "She's sitting on the henhouse roof and she's been there all night! It's not as if she really lives here!"

It was true. The fat, fluffy cat who spent all her time on the farm really belonged to an old lady down the road. Each morning, the old lady brushed Pompom, as she called her cat, and tied a beautiful bow around her neck. Then Pompom proudly walked down the path from the front door and wasn't seen again until suppertime! The old lady had no idea that her cat spent every day on Windytop Farm.

When the other animals heard what Mrs. Speckles was saying, even they were a little concerned. Pompom never spent the night on the farm. She had a cosy bed at home. And her beautiful bow was definitely looking bedraggled this morning.

"There's no doubt about it," hissed Busy Hen to her friend. "She hasn't been home since yesterday."

Just then, Farmer Barnes came out of the farmhouse. He walked through the yard, looking to left and right. When he spotted Pompom he came right over and picked her up.

"I thought you might be here," he said. "Your mistress had to move to a special home, where she can be looked after properly. She can't take you with her, so she has asked me if I will look after you. Of course, I will. But there is one thing. I'm not much use at tying bows, you know, not with these big old fingers. You're a farm cat now. So this will have to go." And he gently pulled Pompom's bow from around her neck.

Of course, the other animals were listening. "What use is she going to be?" hissed Mrs. Speckles. "She's just another mouth to feed."

But just then, one of the little mice who lived in the old henhouse took advantage of the commotion to have a little look around in the new henhouse. The hens spotted him with horror. But so did someone else. In a flash, Pompom dashed into the henhouse and chased the mouse out.

Mrs. Speckles looked at Busy Hen. Busy Hen nodded wisely.

As Pompom strolled back, Mrs. Speckles went boldly forward. "Welcome to Windytop Farm," she said. "We're all very glad you'll be staying with us from now on."

# The Trouble With Denby Dog

Farmer Barnes took good care of all his animals, but Denby Dog was special. He had worked with the farmer for more years than either of them could remember, in sunshine and rain, when the wind was howling around Windytop Farm and when the snow was deep on the ground. Farmer Barnes couldn't imagine life without Denby.

But Denby Dog was getting old. He found it harder to run after the tractor as Farmer Barnes drove out of the yard. His legs felt stiff as he trotted up the lane. Even his bark was not as loud as it used to be.

As winter approached, Farmer Barnes became more and more worried about Denby.

"Old fellow," he said, "the wind is bitter this morning. Why not stay beside the fire or in your kennel in the yard? I can manage without you today."

But the old dog gave Farmer Barnes such a mournful look that he couldn't bear to leave him behind. Later, Denby Dog explained to his friend Biggy Pig how he felt.

"I've been with Farmer Barnes for years, pup and dog," he said. "What if something happened to him away in the fields and I wasn't there to run for help? I'd never forgive myself. No, while there's life in these old bones, I must do my job."

Strangely enough, it was also to Biggy Pig that Farmer Barnes explained his worries that evening. He leaned over the sty wall and scratched Biggy's back.

"It's like this," he said. "Old Denby simply isn't up to the job any more. I've bought a new pup. He'll be arriving tomorrow, but I hate the idea of hurting the old boy's feelings."

Biggy Pig snorted in a comforting sort of way. He felt sure everything would be fine. And it was.

When the new puppy arrived, Denby Dog got straight down to business. "It's high time I retired, young pup," he said. "And now that there'll be someone to follow in my pawprints, I can do it at last. But first, there's a lot I've got to teach you. Follow me now, and leave those chickens alone!"

These days, Denby Dog has a leisurely life, chatting with his friends and lying in the sun. After all, he deserves it.

# Dymphna to the Rescue

Dymphna Duck and Busy Hen were never best friends, but one day something happened that made Busy Hen almost fond of Dymphna. It was during a very busy time on the farm, when Farmer Barnes was hard at work in the fields from morning until night. At such times, he asked his old friend Annie to come each day to take care of the animals.

Now Annie was not the most efficient person. She was likely to forget things and drop things and take twice as long to do a simple job as most people—especially if Farmer Barnes was watching. Busy Hen liked Annie and sympathized. She herself found it very hard to lay an egg if someone was watching her. Besides, Annie was very fond of the animals, and anyone can forgive a knocked-over grain bucket or a late lunch for that.

One morning Farmer Barnes left Annie in charge. "The mechanic is coming to have a look at my old tractor this morning," he said, as he set off to the fields on his new tractor. "Here are the keys. They're the only set I've got, so please don't lose them."

Annie put the keys in her pocket. Then, as Farmer Barnes rumbled away, she set off to fetch Biggy Pig's breakfast. But on the way—and this was typical of Annie—she was sidetracked by the sight of a little duckling sitting forlornly in a puddle in the middle of the yard.

"Poor little thing," said Annie, picking up the duckling. "Can't you find your way back to the pond? Here!" She carefully leaned out into the pond and gently put the duckling onto the water. As she did so, there was a loud splash. The tractor keys had fallen out of her pocket and into the water!

"Oh!" cried Annie. "Oh no!" She hurried off to find the yard broom, to see if she could feel the keys at the bottom of the pond and fish them out. But the bottom of the pond was very muddy. It seemed hopeless.

Busy Hen—as usual—had seen everything that happened. She at once hurried off to find Biggy Pig.

"You like wallowing about in mud, Biggy," she cried. "Can't you find those keys for Annie?"

"My diving days are over," sighed Biggy. "Mud is one thing, but water is quite another."

Busy Hen had run out of ideas, and Annie was close to tears, when Dymphna Duck strolled up with something jangling from her beak. "Is this what you're looking for?" she asked, dropping the keys at Annie's feet.

Annie was so grateful to Dymphna that she gave her the ham and mustard sandwiches from her lunchbox. And it just shows what a nice duck Dymphna is that she shared them all with Busy Hen—although the fact that Annie is as clumsy with mustard as she is with keys might have had something to do with it too!

# Farmer Barnes' Spring Clean

Farmer Barnes is a man who never gives two minutes' thought to the brand of washing powder he uses or whether his kitchen is painted a fashionable shade. As long as something works, he doesn't mind too much what it looks like, which is obvious from his clothes.

But he does like things to be clean, and on a busy farm that's pretty difficult. So that is why, once a year, Farmer Barnes has his big Spring Clean. *Everything* gets cleaned, from the cupboard under the sink to the roof of Biggy Pig's sty.

You've never seen so much washing and brushing, dusting and polishing. All the animals join in. Biggy Pig is good at snuffling dust out of corners, while Busy Hen's beady eyes can spot the tiniest speck of dirt at twenty paces. Dymphna Duck and her friends love anything to do with water, so they splash about in buckets of bubbles all day long. One year, they started to try to shampoo the sheep and had to be stopped by Farmer Barnes.

The last stage of the Spring Clean takes place in the farmhouse. Farmer Barnes carries all the furniture out into the yard and vacuums the house from top to bottom. Then he carries the tables and chairs and beds back into the house and plonks himself down on the sofa. Spring Cleaning is over for another year.

But this year, as Farmer Barnes vacuumed furiously, his old vacuum cleaner making the most extraordinary noises, something dreadful happened. It started to rain! Not just a little gentle shower, but pouring down, splashing on the table and making puddles on the chairs.

"He'll be cross," said Busy Hen anxiously, sheltering under a stool.

"He'll shout and stomp about," agreed Mrs. Speckles. "I don't want to be around when *that* starts."

Then, as suddenly as it began, the rain stopped.

A few minutes later, Farmer Barnes appeared in the yard. He looked at the soggy furniture. His face went red. His forehead furrowed. The animals waited for the second storm of the day.

Then the farmer began to laugh. "This is the cleanest my furniture has *ever* been," he roared. "Let's hope this happens every year!"

# Lala Lamb's Singing Soirée

One morning after breakfast, when the animals were wandering off to do whatever they had planned for the day, they were surprised to hear someone banging a stick on the rain barrel.

"Excuse me!" called a little voice. "Attention, please! Listen!"

It was little Lala Lamb, standing as bold as anything in the middle of the yard. As soon as she was sure all the animals were listening, Lala began her Important Announcement.

"This evening," she said, "I am holding a soirée in the small barn. There will be singing (from me) and all other animals are asked to perform."

Harold the horse asked what everyone else was wondering. "What's a swaray?" he asked. "Will we all have to hold it?"

"No, no," laughed Lala. "A soirée is a kind of musical party. Daphne Duck told me the word. She learnt it from that French hen she knew. Now, I want everyone to be ready at seven o'clock."

By the end of the day, Farmer Barnes was very worried about his animals. He had come across Biggy Pig making the most extraordinary noise behind the pig sty. He didn't know that Biggy was getting ready for the evening.

Later, Farmer Barnes found Busy Hen and half a dozen other hens skipping about in a very strange way. He wondered if a bee was buzzing among them. He didn't know they were preparing for their ballet performance.

As for Harold the horse, Farmer Barnes could hardly believe his ears when he heard Harold mooing and clucking over the stable door. He didn't know that Harold was doing his impressions.

That evening, when Farmer Barnes went in for his supper, everyone gathered in the small barn and the soirée began. It was wonderful! The animals couldn't remember when they had enjoyed themselves so much, even if everyone did think that Biggy's song was an impression of an elephant, and the hens' ballet kicked up so much dust that it was hard to see their footwork.

As a Grand Finale, all the animals sang the Official Farm Song.

Oh, Farmer Barnes he had a farm,
Ee-i-ee-i-o!
And on that farm lived Biggy Pig,
Ee-i-ee-i-o!
With a grunt, snort here,
And a grunt, snort there,
Here a grunt, there a snort,
Everywhere a grunt, snort!
Farmer Barnes he had a farm,
Ee-i-ee-i-o!

Can you sing the rest of the verses?

# Where's Duchess's Hat?

After a few blustery days, Farmer Barnes found he had a lot of repairs to attend to on Windytop Farm. There were tiles missing from the farmhouse roof, large branches to be cleared from the lanes, and one or two fences had fallen down. With so much to think about, it's not surprising that Farmer Barnes wasn't concentrating by the time he was doing his last repair job of the day … putting Scary Scarecrow upright again in the top field. Scary was called Scary because he really wasn't! He was the friendliest-looking scarecrow you've ever seen, and birds from miles around used to come and perch on his hat and shoulders for a chat. Farmer Barnes knew this, but he figured that while birds were chatting, they weren't pecking at his seeds, so that was okay.

Farmer Barnes set Scary Scarecrow firmly upright in the field again and was just about to walk away, when he noticed that Scary no longer had his hat. The farmer looked around. It must have been blown in the wind, but surely it couldn't be far away. Aha! Farmer Barnes spotted a straw hat under the hedge and hurried to scoop it up and plonk it on Scary's head. It looked fine.

But back in the farmyard, someone else was missing a hat! Duchess the cow had lost hers in the wind as well. She sent Delilah the calf and Lala Lamb off to look for it.

Now neither Delilah nor Lala could quite remember what Duchess's hat looked like. They were small animals, and the hat was usually high up on Duchess's head, so it was only when Duchess was lying down that they had a good view. And neither of those young animals was very good at remembering things.

That is why, when Lala and Delilah found a handsome top hat lying under a gate, they brought it straight back to Duchess, full of pride that they had succeeded.

Seeing their eager little faces, Duchess hadn't the heart to be cross. She rather liked her jaunty new headgear, but all the other animals laughed until their sides ached. Lala and Delilah couldn't understand why.

"My dears," smiled Duchess, "you just come with me. We're going to visit a certain scarecrow. He's got something I need, and I believe I have something of his. Fair exchange is no robbery, as they say."

As she passed the duckpond, Duchess had one last look at herself. "Maybe it's not really *me*," she said, "but you'd think the others would realize that a stylish cow like me can carry anything off!"

# The Pie Contest

Farmer Barnes always worked hard, but sometimes he worked too hard. One autumn day, he tried to lift a bag of grain that was simply too heavy—and dropped it on his foot. The hens watched anxiously as he gave a yell and hobbled slowly into the house to call the doctor.

"I don't want you to put any weight on that foot for a week," said the doctor firmly, when she arrived. "Stay in your chair, catch up on some reading, and let your friends take the strain for a while. It's high time you had a rest."

Farmer Barnes grumbled and groaned, but he knew the doctor was right. Anyway, his foot was far too painful to walk on. Farmer Barnes was just beginning to wonder how he would manage as far as food was concerned, when his visitors started to arrive, one by one.

First Mrs. Mannheim from the next farm rushed into the living room.

"I knew you wouldn't be able to get up, so I let myself in," she cried. "And I've brought you one of my extra special chocolate-marshmallow-delight pies. That will keep your spirits up!"

Half an hour later, Miss Florence Fong, from the grocery in town, crept in and peeped around the door.

"I heard about your accident," she said, "and I've made you my lemon-orange-and-pineapple pie, with caramel cream. Everyone seems to like it."

Later that day, Mr. Baxter from the bakery came around with a maple-and-walnut-banana-and-meringue pie. Mrs. Marvel from the local restaurant brought a *tarte aux cerises avec mousse au chocolat blanc* (whatever *that* was), and the doctor herself dropped by with a wholemeal-muesli-oatmeal-and-date pie.

"Sorry!" she laughed. "It's a bit solid. I'm not very good at cooking. But it will do you good!"

That evening, Annie came in from the yard.

"I couldn't get here before," she said, "because there was a lot to do on the farm, but I have made you a pie to keep you going."

Farmer Barnes eyed the ordinary-looking pie.

"What's in it?" he asked.

"I'm afraid it's just a plain apple pie," said Annie. "Oh dear, I can see you've already got lots of beautiful fancy pies."

"And they're *all* too rich and sticky for me," said Farmer Barnes. "A plain apple pie is just what I feel like. I can always rely on you, Annie."

So Farmer Barnes enjoyed his apple pie and felt much better afterwards. As for the other pies, they were very much enjoyed as well … by Biggy Pig, Harold Horse, Lala Lamb, Duchess, Delilah, Mrs. Speckles, Busy Hen, Cackle, Dymphna … in fact, all the animals on Windytop Farm!

# Farmer Barnes Goes to Town

While Farmer Barnes was resting his injured foot, Annie looked after the farm, and she did it very well. If there was anyone who cared as much about the animals as the farmer himself, it was Annie.

"You know," Duchess the cow confessed to Busy Hen, "I wouldn't mind if Farmer Barnes took a little longer to recover. Annie talks to me so nicely during milking."

"I know what you mean," clucked Busy Hen.

One morning, when Annie was feeding the ducks, there came a grumbling and a shouting from Farmer Barnes' open bedroom window.

"Oh, I wonder what the matter is," cried Annie, hoping the farmer hadn't dropped something *else* on his foot.

Dymphna Duck quacked loudly. She knew exactly what was going on. It didn't happen very often, but when Farmer Barnes went to town, he liked to look a bit smarter than usual. And the grumbling and shouting were because he always got cross with the fiddly little buttons on his best shirt. Somehow his big, strong hands weren't made for such things.

At last Farmer Barnes was ready and set off for town.

"Didn't he look smart?" Annie said to Mrs. Speckles. "I expect he was going to the bank."

50

Mrs. Speckles fluttered off to talk to her friend Busy Hen. She believed Farmer Barnes needed a wife, and she felt Mrs. Marchant at the bank was very suitable.

But Busy Hen clucked impatiently. "Mrs. Marchant would be quite out of place on a farm," she said. "Farmer Barnes needs someone like … someone like …" and Busy Hen suddenly looked very thoughtful indeed.

When Farmer Barnes arrived home later that day, he was carrying a big box and looking anxious. He marched straight over to where Annie was clearing out Harold's stable and pushed the box toward her.

"Just wanted to say thank you," he said gruffly, "for all your hard work, you know. Don't know what we'd have done without you."

Annie went pink and peeped into the box. For a few seconds she was speechless. Then she pulled out the prettiest hat you've ever seen.

"I don't know about these things," said Farmer Barnes, looking uncomfortable. "But the lady in the shop said you'd like it."

As Annie at last found her voice, Mrs. Speckles tut-tutted.

"Not at all the right present for Annie," she muttered, remembering Busy Hen's words. "Quite out of place on a farm."

But Busy Hen was doing a little dance of joy all by herself.

"No," she said, "it was *just* right. It was absolutely *perfect.*"

# A Name for a Newcomer

Each year, lots of babies were born on Windytop Farm. Farmer Barnes liked to give names to them all, and he was pretty good at remembering them, too.

But one year, there were so many babies, he had to struggle to think of new names for all of them. There were twenty-four baby ducklings. There were seventeen baby chicks. Add to that nineteen baby lambs, seven little goslings, and Duchess's new calf, and you have a lot of babies.

To make things simpler, Farmer Barnes worked out his own system. He decided to give the chicks names beginning with C, like Charlie and Caroline and Chuckles and Cobweb. The lambs had names beginning with L, like Lucy and Lawrie and Lavender and Lightfoot. The goslings, of course, had names like Gordon and Gerda and George.

It was when he came to the ducklings that Farmer Barnes had problems. He simply could not think of twenty-four names beginning with D, especially as several other animals on the farm, such as Duchess and Delilah, already had D-names.

By the end of the week, after a lot of thought and asking the advice of anyone who came to the farm, Farmer Barnes had twenty-three names, but he was well and truly stuck on the last one. No matter how hard he thought, he simply couldn't come up with another name.

It so happened that the next day, Farmer Barnes' niece paid him a surprise visit, bringing along her baby daughter. All children seemed to like Farmer Barnes. He soon had the little one in fits of giggles. Then he took her and her mother on a tour of the farm.

The baby loved seeing the animals. Last of all, Farmer Barnes took her to the duckpond.

"Here," he said, "is my biggest problem. What would be a good name for a duck, Rosie-Mae?"

Rosie-Mae didn't hesitate. "Duck!" she cried. "Duck! Duck!"

Farmer Barnes laughed out loud. Then he stopped laughing.

"You know," he said, "that's not such a bad idea!"

And that is why, to this day, after he has called Dolores and Deirdre and Darcy and Della and all their brothers and sisters, Farmer Barnes yells "Duck-duck!" and the last little duckling (who's not so little now) comes scuttling along.

# Ready, Set, Go!

With so many baby animals on Windytop Farm, the older animals were busy night and day keeping an eye on them. Even Biggy Pig became accustomed to sleeping with one eye open, in case *another* little duckling dived over the edge of his sty and got stuck in the mud.

As the babies grew older, things got even worse. Although they were much more independent now, they were also much more likely to wander off into the fields— but still not able to find their way home again. Evening after evening, Harold clip-clopped up the lane, calling to all the chicks and ducklings and goslings who had strayed from the farmyard.

One evening, when all the little ones had been rounded up at last, Busy Hen called them together for a Serious Talk. She didn't mince her words. She told them about fast cars, foxes, hawks, and hunters, until they all looked suitably anxious.

"In future," said Busy Hen, "when you want to go somewhere, you must all go together. There's safety in numbers."

After that, it was a common sight to see a long line of baby animals winding its way down the lane and across the fields.

For a while, everything was fine. Then, one evening, the little ones didn't come home! Biggy Pig and Busy Hen set off to find them. They soon came across the little ones far away in the Top Field.

"It's too far to walk home," explained one little duckling. "We're tired. Our little legs won't walk that far. They might even drop off!"

"That's right!" cheeped the others. "We're only small, you know."

"Oh, so you won't be able to take place in the Special Sunset Race, then?" sighed Busy Hen.

"It's a shame," said Biggy Pig.

"What race?" squeaked the little ones. "We're ready! We're ready!"

"The winner is the first one back to the farmyard," said Busy Hen. "Ready? Set! Go!"

Those naughty babies ran off as fast as their little legs would carry them. Busy Hen and Biggy Pig followed them at a more leisurely pace.

"Who won?" asked Biggy, when they reached the yard.

"It was a photo finish!" Harold smiled. "Only we didn't have a photo. We're just going to have to hold the Special Sunset race *every* night until we're sure."

The babies would have cheered, but they were all asleep—every one.

# Biggy Pig's Dancing Lesson

Busy Hen was very busy these days. She was giving all the new chicks and ducklings dancing lessons—and one or two older birds were joining in as well.

"Is it some new fitness craze, Busy?" asked Harold the horse, seeing several ducks bowing their heads this way and that while trying to balance on one foot.

"It's just dancing, Harold," replied Busy Hen. "Further to the left, Dymphna! Don't let that wing droop!"

"But why, Busy Hen? I mean, why is everyone so keen on dancing *now*?"

The dancing teacher looked mysterious. "You never know," she said, "when there might be some kind of ... well ... party or something."

Before long, it was clear to all the animals that the ducks and chicks were becoming very good at their dancing. In fact, lessons drew quite a crowd as Busy Hen put her pupils through their paces.

One morning, just as her class had finished, Busy Hen heard a strange sound coming from the pig sty.

"*Pssssst! Psssst!*"

It was Biggy Pig, trying to attract her attention.

"What's the matter, Biggy?" asked Busy Hen. "Have you lost your voice?"

"No!" whispered the pig. "I just didn't want the other animals to hear. I wanted to talk to you about having dancing lessons."

Busy Hen was surprised, but she tried not to show it.

"Of course, Biggy," she said. "You're welcome to join us any morning."

"I'd be too embarrassed," replied Biggy. "Could I have a private lesson? Say, tonight after dark?"

That night, some extraordinary sounds were heard coming from Biggy's sty. *Bang!* Something hard (like a trotter) hit a feed trough. *Thwack!* Something large (like a bottom) hit a wall. *Ouch!* Something squishy (like a snuffly nose) got too near a flailing foot.

"It's no good, Biggy," said Busy Hen in the darkness. "You can't learn in here. It's too small. Come out into the meadow."

And that is why the smallest chick, opening one sleepy eye at midnight, saw a wonderful sight. It was a pig, dancing in front of the huge harvest moon, and dancing *beautifully*.

# A Wife for Farmer Barnes

These days, Annie seemed to be helping out more and more on the farm. Even when Farmer Barnes' foot was better, he still seemed to need her. The animals were pleased because they liked Annie, and Busy Hen kept her beady eyes open all the time. She didn't want to miss anything exciting. She was certain that Annie and Farmer Barnes should get married, and she felt that it was just a matter of time before the farmer popped the question.

But days passed. Weeks passed. Months passed. The weather grew colder. Annie tramped into the yard early each morning, her breath making clouds in the frosty air.

"If she lived here, she wouldn't have that cold journey down the lane," Busy Hen told Cackle, seeing Annie rubbing her poor red hands together. "I don't know what's the matter with the man," muttered Busy Hen. "He can't see a good thing when it's right in front of his nose."

"Well, it's tricky for a chap," said Cackle. "He's probably afraid she'd say no, and then things on the farm would be difficult. I can understand it. You can't go rushing into these things."

"Well, you would say that, wouldn't you?" retorted Busy Hen. "You never did get up the courage to ask *me* to marry *you*. In the end, I had to do it."

"I can't see Annie saying anything to Farmer Barnes, though," said Cackle. "She's much too ladylike. *Ouch!* Mind what you're doing with your beak, Busy Hen!"

On this occasion, Cackle, as so many times in the past, was completely wrong. One day, Annie marched into the yard carrying a Christmas tree under one arm and a box of trimmings under the other.

"What's that?" asked Farmer Barnes.

"It will be Christmas soon," said Annie, "and I can't bear the thought of you being all by yourself. Christmas is a time for families."

"But…" began Farmer Barnes.

"But you're all on your own, I know," said Annie. "And so am I. I've waited long enough for you to say something, Fred, but I can see I'm just going to have to do it myself. It's high time you got married."

"But…" said Farmer Barnes, looking pink and happy at the same time.

"Yes, I mean me," laughed Annie, but she suddenly wasn't able to say another word.

"Disgraceful!" squawked Mrs. Speckles. "Kissing in the farmyard! Whatever next?"

But Busy Hen was hugging Cackle with delight. "I think it's lovely," she said.

# Tree Trouble

When it is windy on Windytop Farm, as you know, it is *very* windy. One night, the animals covered their ears as they snuggled down in their straw, for a gale was blowing. At first they heard only the howling of the wind. Later there was clattering and clanging as tiles flew from the farmhouse roof and feed troughs tumbled across the farmyard.

The animals didn't feel worried. They were all safe and warm in their stables, or sties, or henhouses, or barns. Busy Hen had helped count the little chicks to make sure they were safe inside—and that took a very long time as they kept scuttling about and hiding in the straw. In the barn, Dymphna was having the same trouble with the ducklings. Poor Dymphna! As well as the noise outside, the ducklings were having a contest to make howling-wind noises!

It wasn't until the next day that the full extent of the storm damage was obvious. A great tree had fallen across the farmyard, only just missing the henhouse and barricading Harold in his stable. Of course, this wasn't the first time that a tree had been blown down on Windytop Farm, but this one had done dreadful damage as it fell.

Farmer Barnes was almost in tears as he looked at the scene in the farmyard. All he could think about was the time it would take and the money it would cost to put everything right again.

Just then Annie arrived and looked around.

"Well," she said, "that *was* lucky!"

"Lucky?" said Farmer Barnes faintly. "How can you call this lucky?"

Annie was smiling. "Not a single animal was hurt," she said, "and neither were you, Fred. I call that very lucky indeed."

Farmer Barnes grinned. "You're right," he said, "as always. Don't worry, Harold, we'll have you free in no time. After all, it's Christmas in a couple of days and we need to be straight by then, don't we?"

# Buzz! Buzz!

Christmas had come at last to Windytop Farm and all the animals were enjoying it enormously. In the morning, Annie put a special treat in each pail of breakfast feed. Harold had some juicy apples. The hens had a special corn and seed mixture. Biggy Pig even had some of Farmer Barnes' own plum pudding!

There were presents, too. Duchess was given a new hat (it was one of Annie's old ones, but it looked very fine trimmed with some new ribbon). Harold became the proud owner of a sign with his name on it above the stable door. There was something for everyone, and the whole farmyard was filled with the sound of happy, chuckling birds and animals.

Only Biggy Pig wasn't feeling on top of the world. At first he thought maybe the plum pudding was disagreeing with him. But after thinking hard about his tummy for a few minutes, he decided that all was well in that department! No, the problem was something else. Gradually, the pig realized what was annoying him. There was a strange buzzing sound very near his left ear.

*Buzz! Buzz! Buzz! Buzz!*

Biggy described the problem to Busy Hen. "It's obvious, Biggy," she replied. "It's a bee!"

Biggy Pig felt relieved for maybe two minutes. Then common sense told him bees simply are not around during the winter. They are snuggled up in their hives somewhere. They are not buzzing around annoying innocent pigs. But if it wasn't a bee, what was it?

Harold the horse, who had clopped by to wish Biggy a Merry Christmas, had another suggestion.

"Buzzing," he said wisely, "is very often caused by something electrical. There are a lot of buzzing things in Farmer Barnes' kitchen. Some of them beep, too. Are you sure it isn't a beeping and not a buzzing you can hear? (Harold himself was a little hard of hearing these days, but then he was a very elderly horse.)

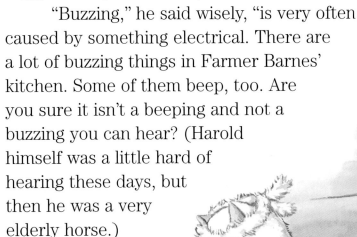

Biggy Pig knew perfectly well whether he was hearing a beeping or a buzzing. Only the holiday season stopped him from telling Harold so rather sharply. Then, just as Biggy felt he couldn't stand the buzzing any longer, along came Pompom the cat.

"So *you've* got it, Biggy!" she cried. "I didn't think pigs were interested in such things."

She pounced into a corner of Biggy's sty and came out with … a clockwork mouse! It had run in under the gate and got stuck!

"Thank you, Pig!" purred Pompom. "And Merry Christmas!"

"And to you, Pompom," replied Biggy. "And a very *peaceful* New Year to all of us," he smiled, looking meaningfully at the mouse.

"*Buzz! Buzz!*" said the mouse. And what *that* meant is anybody's guess!

# Annie Holds the Fort

No sooner had Christmas come and gone than it was lambing time again on Windytop Farm. Night after night, Farmer Barnes stayed up with his sheep, making sure that the little woolly lambs came safely into the world. By the time the last tiny one was trying his first skip and jump on his wobbly little legs, Farmer Barnes was completely exhausted. He felt he wanted to go to bed and not wake up for a week.

"Why don't you have a good night's sleep and visit your sister for a couple of days?" suggested Annie. "I can hold the fort here."

It just shows how tired Farmer Barnes was that he didn't even argue. Next morning, he rattled off in his battered old truck without a murmur.

Annie set to work. She wanted everything to run like clockwork while Farmer Barnes was away.

But everything that *could* go wrong, *did* go wrong. The latch on the pig sty gate didn't catch properly when Annie filled the feed trough, and one little pig escaped. Unfortunately, he ran right into Annie as she was carrying the trays of eggs to the farmhouse. The eggs were smashed and Annie slipped over in the mess, losing one of her boots and falling heavily against the henhouse, making a hole in the roof.

As the hens ran squawking from their breakfast, Scraggles the goat woke up with a start and somehow slipped his chain. He had been tied up because he ate everything and anything that he came across, and he at once set to work on Annie's boot. In the middle of all the commotion, Harold stamped his foot in impatience and lost a shoe.

Busy Hen looked in dismay at the mess. She couldn't bear the idea of Farmer Barnes being cross with Annie, so she had a few sharp words with the other animals. As the hens frowned in concentration, trying to lay an extra morning egg, Scraggles did his duty and ate up all the eggy mess on the ground.

Meanwhile, Annie mended the henhouse roof and called the blacksmith, who not only replaced Harold's shoe but also fixed Scraggle's chain so that the goat couldn't start thinking about an unusual lunch.

When Farmer Barnes came back late the next day, he smiled at the peaceful sight that met his eyes.

"There's never trouble when you're around, Annie," he said. And he didn't hear Annie's reply because the hens suddenly all started talking at once and completely drowned out her words.

As Busy Hen said to Mrs. Speckles, "If Farmer Barnes hears about it, he'll expect us to lay two eggs *every* day, and we can't have that, can we?"

# Don't Be Shy, Little Pig!

Biggy Pig was quite worried about Little Pig. He hoped Little Pig was just going through a phase, but the weeks passed, and things didn't seem to be getting any better.

"I know lots of youngsters are shy," Biggy told his friend Harold the horse, "but Little Pig won't say a word. He just turns pink—I mean, pinker than a pig usually is—and tries to hide his head in the straw. What am I to do with him?"

"It's natural for a youngster to feel shy," said Harold comfortingly. "I remember when I was a foal, I wouldn't say neigh to a goose."

"But Little Pig is growing up," said Biggy Pig. "He should have grown out of his shyness by now."

It was true. Despite his name, Little Pig was now a handsome young pig, almost as big as Biggy himself.

Then, one day, Farmer Barnes brought a new lady pig to Windytop Farm. She was the prettiest little pig any of the animals had ever seen. Her name was Philomena.

It was clear that Little Pig was very taken with Philomena. He gazed at her from afar, sighing and turning rosy pink to the tips of his ears. But did it cure his shyness? Oh no! If anything, matters were worse. When Philomena called a cheery "Good morning, Little Pig!" at breakfast time, Little Pig was so overcome he couldn't eat a thing.

"I simply don't know what to do," Biggy Pig told Harold. "I'm almost ashamed of the young pig. Goodness me, in my young day if a pretty young pig like Philomena had come along, I'd have been chatting to her in no time. Young pigs today just have no get-up-and-go. Those two would make a fine pair, but it's never going to happen."

But Biggy Pig was wrong. The very next day, as Philomena trotted across the farmyard, Biggy Pig was astonished to hear a loud voice just behind him. "Look out!" It was Little Pig! While all the other animals had been busy chatting, Little Pig had seen the ladder propped against the barn wall begin to slip and fall, just as Philomena passed underneath it.

Philomena heard Little Pig's cry and managed to skip away just in time as the ladder came crashing down. Little Pig hurried to her side.

"Are you okay?" he asked. Then he went pink again and couldn't say another word.

"I'm sorry, my dear," said Biggy Pig, coming to join them. "He doesn't mean to be rude."

"Oh, I don't mind at all," said Philomena. "I like strong, silent types like Little Pig. I like them very much."

Well, after that, Little Pig never did say a lot, but he and Philomena have been very happy together ever since. And Biggy Pig has been a little bit quieter than usual…

# The Old Tractor

Farmer Barnes shook his head. "It's no use, Annie," he said. "I must be sensible. This old tractor will always be more trouble than it is worth. I shall call the scrap dealer to come and take it away. We need the money to mend the fences in the Top Field."

"But I know how much that tractor means to you," said Annie. "We can manage. I've a little money of my own saved up…"

"No, Annie," said Farmer Barnes firmly. "I don't want you to spend your savings on the farm. Is that clear? Now, I've made up my mind."

For the next few days, the animals noticed that Farmer Barnes often went to look at the old tractor. He remembered so well how proud he was when his father taught him to drive it. It was then that he decided to follow in his father's footsteps and become a farmer. Selling the tractor was like losing an old friend."

At last the day came when the tractor was taken away. Farmer Barnes hurried off to look at his sheep without saying a word.

A few days later, when Annie and Farmer Barnes were working in the fields, the farmer paused and looked up.

"Annie," he said, "I went to town this morning and bought you a little something. I'm sorry I didn't think of it before."

As she opened the little box, Annie cried out with pleasure. It was an engagement ring with a single shiny stone.

"But how could you afford…?" she began, before a look of understanding crossed her face. "Oh, Fred," she said, "you shouldn't have sold your tractor for me."

"You're worth it," said the farmer, smiling.

"I've bought you a present, too," said Annie, "but it won't arrive until this afternoon."

Farmer Barnes was puzzled, but by three o'clock, when he heard a truck rattling up the lane, he had forgotten all about his present. His eyes opened wide in amazement when he saw on the back of the truck—his old tractor!

"You didn't say I couldn't spend my savings on *you*, Fred," said Annie.

But Farmer Barnes hardly heard her. His eyes were brimming with all the tears he had not cried when the tractor was taken away.

I'm a lucky man, Annie, was all he said, as he stomped over to greet the driver. And his voice sounded even gruffer than usual.

# Moonlight Serenade

Windytop Farm is always a busy place, but in the days leading up to Farmer Barnes' wedding, it was incredibly busy. Although the ceremony was taking place in the nearby town, all the guests were coming back to the farm afterwards.

An enormous marquee was put up in the home field. Although Farmer Barnes was not a man to spend money idly, he was determined to have a wonderful wedding. As he told Biggy Pig one morning, "I only intend to do this once in my life, so I'm going to do it properly. And anyway, I want Annie to have a lovely day."

All week people were coming and going—with food, flowers, presents, and mysterious packages of all kinds. The animals tried not to get in the way but they were curious, so Busy Hen and some of her friends fluttered here and there and reported back to the others on what was going on.

70

"Everything's ready," Busy Hen told them as the sun went down the day before the wedding. "I even saw Farmer Barnes' special suit arrive. Nothing can go wrong now."

But that night, as Busy Hen watched the lighted windows of the farmhouse, she began to worry. Farmer Barnes had not gone to bed. She could see him pacing up and down inside.

"He needs a good night's sleep," said Busy Hen. "Whatever can be the matter?"

"I know what it is," replied Cackle, unexpectedly. "It's a worrying thing, getting married. Farmer Barnes is anxious about tomorrow, that's all. He'll be fine if he once gets to sleep."

"Then we must help him," said Busy Hen. And she called together all the animals she could find and ushered them underneath the farmhouse windows. "Lala Lamb will sing the solo," she said. "Now, everyone, as softly as you can. One, two, three!"

The animals sang beautifully, but Farmer Barnes put his head out of the window almost at once.

"What's that noise?" he cried. "I've got to get to sleep, you know!"

Lala looked concerned, but Busy Hen smiled.

"He'll feel better now he's had a shout at someone," she said.

And she was right. The farmhouse lights went out, one by one, and everything was quiet on Windytop Farm.

# A Windytop Wedding

Farmer Barnes was up bright and early on his wedding morning. It didn't matter if it *was* a special day, the animals still needed to be fed, the eggs had to be collected, and the cows were waiting to be milked.

All the animals made a special effort. Farmer Barnes had never seen so many eggs from his hens, and he filled almost twice as many churns as usual with milk. This really was a special day.

By half past nine, all the important jobs were done, and Farmer Barnes went into the farmhouse to get ready. When he came out again, he was hardly recognizable. All the animals watched as he climbed into his old truck and rumbled off down the lane.

"He's gone!" cried Busy Hen, scuttling round the barnyard as fast as she could. "We haven't got much time. Come on!" And all the animals dashed into action. The hens fluttered off to collect wild rose-petals from the hedges. Pompom the cat, who had clever little paws, tied bows on all the lady animals and helped Duchess to get her hat straight. Biggy Pig put on his biggest Best-of-Show ribbon, and Harold stood patiently as Pompom braided and decorated his mane.

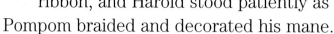

When everyone was ready, the animals hurried to hide, for they could hear the sound of a battered old truck coming down the lane.

The truck stopped in front of the farmhouse. Farmer Barnes got out, with a big smile on his face, and walked around to open the other door.

"He's never done that before," whispered Biggy Pig to Dymphna Duck.

"He's never been married before," whispered Dymphna. "Oh, look!"

The new Mrs. Barnes was getting out of the truck, and she looked absolutely beautiful.

"Everyone else will be here in a minute, darling," said Farmer Barnes, "but I'm looking forward to life being just like this. Just you and me and Windytop Farm."

"I may cry!" Duchess sniffed.

"Not yet, Duchess," called Busy Hen. "Come on, everyone. Now!"

The animals rushed out to cheer, quacking, clucking, mooing, snuffling, and baa-ing, while Dymphna and her friends flew up to scatter rose petals all over the happy couple.

"No, Fred," smiled Annie, "just you and me and Windytop Farm and all our friends who live here."

"Now I *am* going to cry," said Duchess. And she did.

# Arthur's Ark

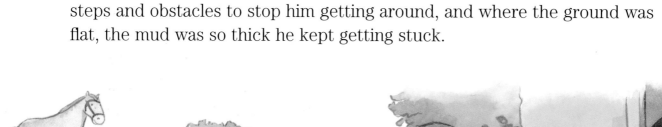

One spring day, a party of schoolchildren visited Windytop Farm. Their teacher had arranged it with Fred and Annie Barnes a few weeks before.

"The only thing I'd say," warned Farmer Barnes on the telephone, "is that they must wear boots. The barnyard can get very muddy at this time of year."

The teacher said she understood, and the arrangements were made.

On the day of the visit, it was cloudy and quite cold. As Farmer Barnes had feared, there was a lot of mud everywhere. He was pleased to see, as the children climbed out of their minibus, that they all had sensible boots on their feet—except for one little boy.

"Arthur joined us from another school this week," said the teacher. "He's a wizz with his wheelchair and he's really looking forward to seeing the animals."

But Arthur didn't see very much of the farm. There were all sorts of steps and obstacles to stop him getting around, and where the ground was flat, the mud was so thick he kept getting stuck.

"I'm so very sorry," said Annie. "We'll have to change things around here. Everyone should be able to visit Windytop Farm and see everything they want to see."

"It is a shame," said the teacher. "Arthur loves animals so much."

That night, as they had their supper, Farmer Barnes told Annie, "I feel badly about that boy. I'm going to make him a present to show how sorry we are."

So Farmer Barnes went into his workshop and got out his tools. A couple of days later, he carried lots of little wooden animals and a wooden ark into the farmhouse.

"I thought we could paint these after supper," he told Annie.

"They look lovely, Fred," said Annie.

Next morning, the whole set was ready. There were elephants, giraffes, polar bears, lions, tigers, and crocodiles. Annie packed them up and took them down to the school for Arthur.

But when Arthur opened the package, although he looked pleased, he was a little disappointed too.

"Thank you very much," he said, "but it was pigs and sheep and things I really wanted to see."

When Annie told Farmer Barnes, he understood at once. "The boy is quite right," he said, and he hurried off to make beautiful little models of all the farm animals he could think of.

This time, Arthur beamed with pleasure.

"It's almost as good as seeing around the farm," he said.

"And we'll make sure you can do just that next time," promised Annie. "See you then!"

# The Moon Pig

Biggy Pig was waiting patiently for his breakfast one morning when he noticed the sun was already peeping over the barn roof. Biggy's tummy felt odd. It knew perfectly well that when the sun was as high as *that* in the sky, it was well past breakfast time. Where was Annie? It was very strange.

A few minutes later, he heard the clanking of buckets, and Farmer Barnes looked over the door of the sty.

"Here's your breakfast, old friend," he said. "Sorry it's a bit late, but I don't want Annie overdoing things."

Biggy might have thought that was strange too, but he already had his head deep in the feed trough and he didn't hear a word.

Little Pig was not so greedy. He heard everything Farmer Barnes said, and later, when Biggy was resting his (very full) tummy, he began to wonder out loud about what was happening on Windytop Farm.

"It's very mysterious," said Little Pig, "and my dear Philomena agrees with me. There have been several strange happenings recently. Lots of the animals have noticed it."

"Like what?" yawned Biggy, thinking it was time for his morning nap.

"Like the eggs not being collected on time," said Little Pig. "Like Annie not coming to scratch my back like she used to do. Like the farmyard being so untidy. Like Annie wearing Farmer Barnes' clothes—I think that's very odd."

"I think she's got too fat for her clothes," said Biggy Pig, who knew a thing or too about getting fat and thought it was the best thing that could happen to anyone—or any pig.

"I still think it's strange," said Little Pig. "But there are odd things that are really spooky, too. Like the Moon Pig."

"The Moon Pig?" asked Harold the horse, who had been shamelessly eavesdropping during the pigs' conversation.

"Yes," said Little Pig, pleased to have a bigger audience. "When the Moon Pig turns blue, that means strange and wonderful things are going to happen. And the Moon Pig has been blue all this week."

"It's just the time of year," said Harold. "The moon always looks blue around now. And anyway, I don't know what you mean about the Moon Pig. It's obviously a horse in the moon. Everyone knows that."

But that night, Little Pig gazed up at the moon and whispered to himself. "I don't care what Harold says. Something strange and wonderful *is* going to happen. And it's going to happen soon."

# You'll Never Believe It!

One morning, Little Pig scuttled around the farmyard as fast as his little trotters would carry him. He skidded to a halt in front of Dymphna the duck.

"I know what it is!" he panted. "I know why everything's been strange around here recently. I just overheard Annie and Farmer Barnes talking. You'll never believe it!"

"Well, what is it?" asked Dymphna crossly.

Little Pig whispered in her ear.

"You're right," said Dymphna. "I don't believe a word of it."

So Little Pig hurried on to have a word with Duchess the cow.

"You'll never believe it," he squeaked. And he stood on his hind legs to whisper in Duchess's ear.

"Nonsense, young pig!" cried Duchess.

Little Pig scampered off. He found Scraggles the goat happily munching.

"You'll never believe it!" said Little Pig. "Just listen."

"You silly pig," said Scraggles. "That's ridiculous."

Feeling pretty desperate now, Little Pig ran to find Harold the horse.

"You'll never believe it!" he yelled. And he told Harold exactly what he had told the others.

"I'm quite sure that can't be right," said Harold. "And you shouldn't spread such stories."

Little Pig was sitting sadly on a bale of
straw when Busy Hen came by.

"What's the matter, Little Pig?" she asked.

"I know a really big secret," said Little Pig,
"and I've told everyone, and they don't believe it."

"Well, you haven't told me," said Busy Hen.

So Little Pig whispered his secret. And
Busy Hen looked thoughtful for a moment.

"I know," she said. "I've known for ages.
I don't know why the other animals are so
silly. Don't worry, Little Pig. All we have to
do is wait. Then everyone will see."

Three weeks later, in the middle of the
night, there was a lot of going back and forth at
Windytop Farm. Then, through the still night air,
came a strange sound.

"It's a baby!" cried Harold.

"But…" quacked Dymphna the duck.

"But…" mooed Duchess the cow.

"But …" bleated Scraggles the goat.

"But… " neighed Harold the horse.

"BUT…" they cried together, "that
means you were right, Little Pig. And it's
*wonderful* news."

And as Little Pig and Busy Hen smiled at
each other above the excited chattering, Farmer
Barnes leaned out of the bedroom window with a
very small person in his arms and said,

"*Ssssssssssssssssssssshhhhhhhhhhhhh!*"

# Index of Themes